Some Smug Slug

by Pamela Duncan Edwards
illustrated by Henry Cole

HarperCollins*Publishers*

The illustrations in this book were painted with acrylic paints and
colored pencils on Arches Hot Press watercolor paper.

S
O
M
E

S
M
U
G

S
L
U
G

Text copyright © 1996 by Pamela Duncan Edwards
Illustrations copyright © 1996 by Henry Cole
Manufactured in China. All rights reserved.
For information address HarperCollins Children's Books,
a division of HarperCollins Publishers,
10 East 53rd Street, New York, NY 10022.

Library of Congress Cataloging-in-Publication Data
Edwards, Pamela.
    Some smug slug / by Pamela Duncan Edwards ; illustrated by Henry
Cole.
        p.   cm.
    Summary: A smug slug that will not listen to the animals around it
comes to an unexpected end.
    ISBN 0-06-024789-4. — ISBN 0-06-024792-4 (lib. bdg.) —
    ISBN 0-06-443502-4 (pbk.)
    [1. Slugs (Mollusks)—Fiction.   2. Animals—Fiction.]   I. Cole, Henry,
ill.   II. Title.
PZ7.E263658o   1996   94-18682
[E]—dc20   CIP
                                                                      AC

Typography by Elynn Cohen
❖
12 13 SCP 20 19 18 17 16 15 14 13 12 11

For dear Peter,
who would have laughed.
—P.D.E.

Stephen—Scooby!
—H.C.

One summer Sunday
while strolling on soil,

4

with its antennae signaling,
a slug sensed a slope.

5

Slowly the slug started
up the steep surface,
stringing behind it
scribble sparkling like silk.

"Stop!" screamed a sparrow,
shattering the silence.

9

"Save him!" shrieked a spider,
scurrying down its strand.

11

"Silly," sighed a swallowtail,
swooshing through the spice bush.

"Saphead!" snickered a skink
as its sapphire tail swished.

With a shrug of its shoulders, on the slug sauntered. With a swagger it slithered up, up the slant.

"Show-off," scolded a squirrel,
storing nuts for the season.

16

"So sad," squealed a stink bug, shivering on a stem.

17

For one single second
in a sunbeam it slumbered;
its sleek skin was soft like
shantung.

19

Seldom swerving or straggling
or swaying or skewing,

the smug slug shambled on.

Struggling up to the summit,
the slimy slug smiled
a self-satisfied smile.

In spite of sinister signs,
it showed no suspicion,

until something shifted,
and shuddered and shook.

26

That sly, slippery slope
was simply a sham.

Such a shock, such a shame.

Such a succulent slug!

Somewhere in this story,
did you see a skunk, a snake, a salamander,
and two snails spying on the slug?

Also hidden in each picture is an "S" shape.
Can you spot it?